FRANKIE'S MAGIC FOOTBALL

FRANKIE'S MAGIC FOOTBALL

MAMMOTH MAYHEM
FRANK LAMPARD

LITTLE, BROWN BOOKS FOR YOUNG READERS
www.lbkids.co.uk

LITTLE, BROWN BOOKS FOR YOUNG READERS

First published in Great Britain in 2017 by Hodder and Stoughton

1 3 5 7 9 10 8 6 4 2

Copyright © Lamps On Productions Ltd, 2016

The moral right of the author has been asserted.

A CIP catalogue record for this book
is available from the British Library.

ISBN 978-1-51020-112-5

Typeset in Cantarell by M Rules
Printed and bound in Great Britain by
Clays Ltd, St Ives plc

The paper and board used in this book are made
from wood from responsible sources.

Little, Brown Books for Young Readers
An imprint of
Hachette Children's Group
Part of Hodder and Stoughton
Carmelite House
50 Victoria Embankment
London EC4Y 0DZ

An Hachette UK Company
www.hachette.co.uk

www.hachettechildrens.co.uk

*To my mum Pat, who encouraged me
to do my homework in between kicking
a ball all around the house, and is still
with me every step of the way.*

*Welcome to a fantastic
Fantasy League – the greatest
football competition ever held
in this world or any other!*

*You'll need four on a team,
so choose carefully. This is a lot
more serious than a game in the
park. You'll never know who your
next opponents will be, or
where you'll face them.*

*So lace up your boots, players,
and good luck! The whistle's
about to blow!*

The Ref

PART ONE

CHAPTER 1

"Hurry up!" Frankie's dad called up the stairs. "Charlie's here!"

Frankie looked out of his bedroom window. Sure enough, a people carrier was parked in the street outside, and Frankie could see Louise and Charlie sitting in the back with the windows wound down. Charlie's dad and Louise's sat in the front together. The boot was loaded up with tents and sleeping bags, and there was an open roofbox on top.

Frankie waved to his friends. He'd been looking forward to this weekend for ages — it was Father's Day, and they were going camping with just their dads. The sun was out, they'd have a barbecue, and explore the woods together. Everything was perfect ...

"Hey, Frankenstein — get a move on," came a voice from the bedroom door. "You move slower than a Liverpool defender with lead boots."

Well, almost everything.

Frankie's brother Kevin barged in,

holding a rucksack over his shoulder and chewing on gum.

"Just making sure I've got everything I need," said Frankie, as he began to place things in his own bag. Torch, compass, waterproofs, insect repellent ...

"We're only going to a campsite," said Kevin. "Not the Amazon rainforest."

Frankie wished he had some *Kevin* repellent. "Doesn't hurt to be prepared," he said. "Tell Dad I'll be down in two minutes."

As Kevin turned, he pointed at Frankie's wardrobe. "Aren't you taking your little toy?" he asked.

Frankie saw the magic football sitting on top. Though it looked very sorry for itself – leather peeling, half deflated – both Frankie and his brother knew it had remarkable powers to open doorways to other worlds.

"Keep your voice down or Mum will hear," he said. Only Frankie and his friends, plus Kevin, were aware of the football's secret. "And no, I'm leaving it here. Dad wants us to enjoy this weekend together."

Kevin took out his chewing gum, stuck it on Frankie's wardrobe door, and stalked off.

Max the dog looked the up from the end of the bed, and whined.

"I know, boy," said Frankie. "Maybe some fresh air will do him good."

With his things packed, he headed downstairs. His mum was waiting by the front door. She and the other mums were heading off for a weekend too, at a local spa. She kissed Frankie on the head. "Look after your dad, won't you?" she said.

Frankie grinned and ran outside. His dad threw his rucksack into the roofbox and Frankie scrambled in next to his friends. Max hopped up on the seat beside him, and Frankie made sure his harness was fastened. He frowned. Where was Kevin?

At that moment, his brother came striding from the house.

"You look pleased with yourself," said his dad.

Kevin packed his bag up top as well. "Just looking forward to a night in the great outdoors," he said.

It was a long drive to the campsite, and when they eventually arrived it was almost 4pm. Charlie's dad pulled off the main road past a sign that read STONE CIRCLE CAMP AND CARAVAN PARK.

"Funny name," muttered Kevin.

Louise looked up from her book. "Not really. There's an ancient circle of stones on the hill above the site. No one really knows who built it, or why, but archaeologists think it's thousands of years old."

"Sounds boooring," said Kevin.

No it doesn't, thought Frankie. *It sounds mysterious and exciting.* He couldn't wait to go and take a look.

"Maybe it was a football pitch!" said Charlie. "Like the first stadium."

Louise giggled. "It was long time before football was even invented, Charlie."

He looked troubled. "What did kids play, then?"

Before anyone could answer, Charlie's dad swerved into a space by the edge of the forest and stopped.

"This is our spot," he said.

"I want something to eat," grumbled Kevin, climbing out.

"First we put up the tents," said their dad.

They'd brought two tents, one for the dads and one for the kids. The dads' one looked pretty old and smelly – Charlie's father had had it since he'd been trekking as a young man. It weighed a tonne and seemed very complicated to put up. But Louise had brought her older sister's new tent for her friends. It had bendy poles and water-resistant, breathable fabric. By the time they'd finished pegging it out and laid their camping mats and sleeping bags inside, the dads were still puzzling over the instructions for their tent. Max lay on the grass, scratching himself.

"We'd better give them a hand," said Frankie.

"No way," muttered Kevin. He was sitting on the ground, munching a chocolate bar. He didn't offer any to the others.

With everyone apart from Kevin helping, they soon got the other tent up. There was only one more thing to do, which was to peg out several ropes that were attached to the tent. The ropes were called "guys".

Frankie was happy to stay with his dad while Charlie's dad and Louise's set up the barbecue. Louise and Charlie went to explore the games room on the campsite.

"The guys help keep the tent stable if it's windy," explained Frankie's dad. "Help me tie loops at the end for the pegs."

Frankie wasn't sure how. He'd never been very good at knots.

"Come, I'll show you," said his dad. "It's called a slipknot – sort of like a mini lasso."

Frankie watched closely and saw that it was easy, really. By the time they were done, Frankie could smell the barbecue smoking and Louise and Charlie came running back.

"There's table football!" said Louise. "Maybe we can arrange a tournament with the other kids on the campsite."

"Won't you have to take your gloves off to grip the handles properly?" Frankie asked Charlie.

His friend swallowed. "I didn't think of that. Maybe I'll just watch."

Louise laughed. Charlie didn't take his gloves off to eat, to sleep, or even in the bath if he could help it. "I think you could make an exception," she said.

"Table football is rubbish anyway," said Kevin. "The real thing is *so* much more . . . interesting."

Frankie saw his brother approaching, and he was holding something behind his back. Frankie had a sinking feeling. He suddenly remembered how his brother had emerged from the house after everyone else, with that smug grin on his face.

"You didn't bring it . . ." he said.

Kevin's eyebrow arched. "Bring what?" he said innocently.

"I told you not to," said Frankie. "You stole it from my room!"

Kevin brought the magic football in front of him. Louise gasped and Charlie threw a panicked glance at Frankie. He knew exactly what they were thinking. *In Kevin's hands, that*

football could get us into all sorts of trouble!

"If you want it, come and get it," said his brother slyly.

And with those words, he turned and ran away into the forest.

CHAPTER 2

"After him!" said Frankie.

Max barked and scampered off in pursuit, followed by Frankie and his friends.

"Where are you lot rushing off to?" called Louise's dad. "We'll be eating soon."

"Football!" yelled Louise. "Back in a bit!"

"Save me a sausage!" added Charlie.

They ran between the trees, jumping over fallen logs. Kevin was quick, though, and he was already way ahead. Then Frankie lost sight of him among the trees.

"Split up!" panted Frankie. "We'll cut him off."

They separated. It was tough going over the forest floor, and Frankie tripped a couple of times on tree roots. Though his chest burned from climbing, his anger drove him on. His brother couldn't stop interfering. Would he ever learn his lesson?

"He's over here!" called Charlie, to Frankie's right.

Frankie veered that way and saw Louise closing in, too. He saw Kevin climbing over a stile at the upper edge of the forest, football tucked under his arm. Frankie vaulted over, followed by Max and the others. Then they were running through a sloping meadow, and he could see he was gaining on his brother. Kevin turned back to look, then suddenly fell down, hard, with a cry. The football flew into the air.

Frankie reached the brow of the hill, and found his brother lying on the ground, grimacing and clutching his foot. He'd tripped over a rock sticking up out of the ground.

"Are you all right?" Frankie asked.

Kevin's face was red and sweating. "I think I've broken my toe!" he said.

Frankie resisted the urge to blame his brother.

Louise and Charlie arrived, breathing hard. Louise crouched down, and cradled Kevin's foot. Kevin winced. "It's probably just

a nasty knock," she said. "There's some ice back at the campsite."

"Who left that rock there anyway?" said Kevin. He kicked it grumpily with his other foot.

"Who knows," said Charlie. "But I think it's been there a while."

Frankie saw what he meant — the rock was mottled and mossy, with grass springing up around its edges. The stone was just one of dozens, all laid out in a huge circle. Some were bigger than others, coming almost up to his waist, while some had fallen over and lay on their sides. The whole thing was about thirty paces across.

"Looks like we've found the stone circle," he said.

"It's magnificent!" said Louise. "Can you imagine how long they've stood here on this hill? What a magical place!"

"Yeah, right," said Kevin.

"Can you stand up?" asked Frankie.

Kevin hobbled to standing, with a grimace. He gingerly put some weight on his foot.

"Doesn't look that bad after all," said Charlie, rolling his eyes. "Anyway, where's the football?"

The grass inside the stone circle was quite long, so they all began to search together. Frankie thought

24

it hadn't gone far, but he couldn't find it anywhere. Max trotted this way and that, just his wagging tail showing above the grass.

Suddenly, with a yelp, he dropped out of sight.

"Max?" called Frankie, rushing over. He stopped suddenly. Where Max had been a moment ago, the grass had vanished, leaving only a black hole in the ground. "Oh no!"

"What is it?" asked Louise, and she and Charlie came towards him. They gasped when they saw the black circle on the ground. It looked like an open manhole cover, descending into a bottomless abyss. Kevin began to hobble in his direction, too.

Frankie recognised a portal when he saw one. The football must have made it. Scanning around, he realised it was right in the middle of the stone circle.

"Where does it go?" asked his brother.

"Who knows?" said Frankie. "But Max is down there, so I'm going after him."

"Me too!" said Charlie.

"And me," added Louise.

They all looked at Kevin. "No chance," he said.

"*You* caused this mess," said Louise, through gritted teeth.

Kevin began to back away quickly. "But my toe . . ."

"It doesn't seem to be bothering you much anymore," said Charlie

"Let him go," said Frankie. He glared at his brother. "Don't tell dad *anything*," he said. "I don't want this to ruin his trip."

Kevin nodded, pale-faced.

Frankie looked at his friends. "Ready?"

"Ready," they repeated.

They linked hands and jumped into the portal together.

Frankie expected to fall, but it

was more like taking a small step. In a flash of light, everything changed.

Well, some things were the same.

He was still standing in the stone circle, but the grass was short and the stones themselves looked much cleaner, almost as if they'd been recently scrubbed and polished. Tiny speckles of quartz glinted under the surface. All the stones were upright, too.

But beyond the edge of the stone circle, the landscape was completely different. There were trees everywhere, stretching into the distance, and a river flowed through a valley below where before it had

been a road. He couldn't see a single house, or building, or car, or telegraph pole, or pylon. Every sign of modern life had vanished. The only thing that was the same was the sun in the sky. It was sinking towards the distant hills.

"What happened to our clothes?" asked Charlie.

Frankie looked down. His football shirt had gone, replaced with what looked like a fur tunic, tied with a strip of leather around the middle. Louise and Charlie were dressed the same. Their feet were bare.

"I think we've gone back in time," said Louise. "A *long way* back in time."

CHAPTER 3

Frankie heard Max barking, and his dog came running out of the bushes, tail wagging.

"Where'd it go? Where'd it go?" he panted.

"Where did what go?" asked Frankie. He was used to Max being able to talk on their adventures.

"The *rabbit!*" said Max. "I'm sure it came this way."

"Forget about the rabbit," said Frankie. "We need to work out where we are."

"I think it's prehistoric times," said Louise. Her eyes lit up. "Maybe we're going to meet the people who actually made this stone circle."

Charlie walked over to the edge and leaned over to pick something up. "At least we've got this," he said, holding the magic football. "Maybe we should just go back now, before we get into trouble."

Frankie gazed around. He'd have loved to stay, but their dads would get worried if they were missing too long, and who knew what Kevin would say?

"I think Charlie's right," he said.

"What about the rabbit?" asked Max, looking up hopefully.

Louise crouched to stroke his head. "We have rabbits back in our own time," she said.

The bushes beside the stone circle rustled. "Father?" came a voice.

Frankie and his friends froze as a boy carrying a spear emerged from the undergrowth. He too was dressed in animal skins, and had messy brown hair and tanned scrawny limbs. Frankie guessed he was ten or eleven.

"Who are you?" asked the boy. "Have you seen my father?"

Frankie shook his head, and introduced his friends.

"That's a strange-looking wolf," said the boy, pointing his spear at Max.

"He's not a wolf," said Frankie. "He's a dog. What's your name?"

"Cywan," said the boy. "What's a dog?"

"We're like wolves, but much cleverer," said Max.

Cywan leapt back, alarmed. He looked at the stones of the circle. "This talking animal must be from the spirit world!" He fell to his knees. "Spirits, help me find my father and I will make offerings."

Frankie walked towards him, and helped him up. "We're not from the spirit world," he said, "but we'll help you."

The light dipped a little as the sun began to disappear over the horizon.

"We must return to the cave," said Cywan. "Night comes soon, and it will be dangerous."

"Dangerous, how?" said Charlie, eyes wide.

"Wolves hunt these hills at night," said Cywan. "Come, follow me."

Frankie wasn't sure at first. What about getting home? He looked at his wrist to check his watch, but of course it had vanished.

Oh well, we won't stay too long, he thought. *And this stone circle's not going anywhere.*

So he walked with the others after the boy, away from the circle. A distant howl echoed through the hills.

"I don't like the sound of that," Max whined.

Frankie shuddered. *Nor do I.*

Cywan led them down a narrow track down between the trees.

Soon Frankie smelled cooking meat, and woodsmoke. They emerged into a clearing at the bottom of a rocky slope. A number of people sat in front of a cave mouth, around a fire. One woman who looked very old was stitching animal skins, two girls of about sixteen were stirring a pot and turning a spit over the fire, and a boy of about five or six was doing a handstand in front of a woman who Frankie guessed was his mother. They all went silent when they saw Frankie and his friends.

"I found these strangers in the stone circle," said Cywan.

"How dare they!" said one of the girls.

"What tribe are they from?" asked the other.

"Their creature talks!" said Cywan. "I think they're from the spirit world."

The little boy came up cautiously and poked Charlie's glove. "He has the paws of a bear!"

"And was there any sign of your father?" asked the younger woman.

"No," said Cywan sadly. "Not even any tracks. But with the spirit creature to guide us . . ."

"Don't be a fool," said the girl stirring the pot. "This is no spirit animal. It's some sort of runt wolf."

"Excuse me!" said Max. "I am no runt."

Everyone gasped and the old woman began to fiddle nervously with a necklace of beads.

"I told you – he's a spirit," said Cywan. "Maybe even the *Great Spirit.*"

"Perhaps we should offer food to our guests," said the elderly woman. "There is plenty to go around."

"Thank you," said Frankie. He was starting to think the football had brought them here to help find Cywan's father, but he needed time to come up with a plan. He learned the names of the others — the old woman was Olsa, Cywan's grandmother. The girls were Jeri and Tash, the youngest boy Rai, and his mother Karla.

The meat on the spit was a deer, he thought, and there was some sort of stew made with grains and vegetables that they drank from wooden bowls. It was delicious. There were sour berries too, and fish that had been baked in a wooden vessel beside the fire. Louise blew on her fingers as she tried to eat it without a knife and fork. The girls were whispering to one another and laughing. One had a bow looped over her shoulder and quiver of arrows on her back. As he looked more closely, Frankie realised the tips were sharpened pieces of flint.

"There's no metal anywhere!" he said to Louise.

"I think this is the Stone Age," she replied. "Maybe ten or twenty thousand years ago!"

Frankie chewed the venison. The football had once taken them to the land of the dinosaurs, millions of years back, so anything was possible.

"Tell us what happened to your father," he said to Cywan.

The boy had hardly eaten, he realised. "He went out hunting yesterday morning," said Cywan. "Sometimes he will be away a whole day, but never overnight." He looked down, and Frankie saw a tear falling from his eye. "He could be anywhere."

All the people around the fire looked desperate, like a team three-nil down at half-time.

"We will find him," said Frankie, trying to sound hopeful. "Tomorrow, we will begin the search."

"With the Great Spirit to guide you," added Max, chewing on a bone. Another howl carried over the night, and Max trembled. "Is anyone else cold?" he said.

"Let's go inside," said one of the girls.

Frankie had been wondering what they'd find inside the cave, and it was more luxurious than he was expecting. The girls threw wood on another fire, and there were furs on the ground, with rushes underneath for padding. As the flames began to throw orange flickers across the walls, he saw they were decorated with paintings

in reds and greens and blues.
There were animals like horses and
deer and bears, as well as human
handprints.

"They're beautiful!" said Louise.

The little boy, Rai, approached
with a small wooden pot filled with
thick red paint. He placed his hand
in, then reached up and left a print
on the wall. Then he offered it to
Frankie and his friends. One by
one, they placed their hands in and
left their marks. Charlie was last,
looking uncertain, but eventually
placed his glove in the paint and left
a larger, smudged print.

"That's enough now," said

Cywan's mother, Karla. "We must all rest."

Frankie was given a bed, and settled down among the warm furs. As he did, he noticed a huge ivory horn hanging from the wall.

"Wow!" he said. "Is that from an elephant?"

The old woman, Cywan's grandmother Olsa, shuffled over. "I have never heard of this elephant creature. It is the tusk of a bull mammoth, hunted by my own father and his tribe. We blow it when we want to summon each other, or when there is danger."

Frankie didn't feel very tired as everyone lay down to sleep. He'd seen mammoths in books, but the horn was enormous – he simply couldn't imagine one in the flesh. He looked across and saw that Cywan wasn't asleep, either. The boy was clutching piece of leather in his hand, his brows knitted with worry.

Frankie hoped he could help, but what chance did they have?

Despite his fears, it wasn't long before the flickering fire and the soft breathing all around pulled him into a slumber.

CHAPTER 4

When Frankie opened his eyes, it was dawn and he could smell baking bread. The others stirred as well, and they emerged from the cave, blinking into the pale morning.

Cywan's grandmother was already up, baking flatbreads on a stone laid over the fire.

Cywan was clutching his spear,

ready to go. "I told you, we don't need food."

"Nonsense," said the old woman. "A decent breakfast will help you search. The spirit guide has already eaten."

Max was licking his teeth, looking pleased with himself. "I could eat another," he muttered hopefully. "Keep my spirits up and all. Get it? Spirits?"

No one looked very amused.

Frankie didn't want to stick around either, but Olsa insisted. From a stone jar she took out sections of sticky honeycomb and wrapped the bread around it,

50

handing them one each. As Frankie took a bite, the sweetness exploded in his mouth.

"Come on," said Cywan. "Let's get spears for you."

One of the older girls carried three spears in her arms. Frankie took one, weighing it in his hand. He had no idea what he was supposed to use it for, or even if he could throw it straight. He hoped he didn't have to.

"Good luck!" called Cywan's mother. "Bring your father home, son."

With Max scampering at their side, they took the track back to the stone circle.

"What's it actually for? The circle, I mean," asked Charlie as they passed.

Cywan, Frankie noticed, led them around the edge rather than through the middle. "It's a place we can talk to the spirits," said the boy. "We leave offerings, and at special times of the year all the tribes gather here."

"Did you build it?" asked Louise.

"Oh, no," said Cywan matter-of-factly. "It has been here since the spirits left to live in the sky."

They set off through the trees for what seemed like about twenty minutes, then emerged over a vast, rolling plain filled with copses of trees and ponds and outcrops of rock. Apart from a few birds, and a squirrel scampering through the branches, Frankie hadn't seen any animals, but there were lots of droppings on the ground. He did his best to avoid them, though his feet were already filthy from walking across the bare earth and tree roots.

"Father often came to the plain to hunt," said Cywan.

"Should we split up?" asked Louise. "It might be quicker."

"Too dangerous," said Cywan.

"A wolf pack would attack a single person, but not a group. Big cats sometimes come this way too."

"I'm not scared of big cats," said Max.

Louise leaned close to him. "I think he might be talking about sabre-toothed tigers," she muttered. "You know, as big as horses, with teeth longer than you are tall."

"Oh," said Max, tail drooping.

Frankie noticed that Cywan was still holding the piece of leather from the night before, only now it was hanging from his belt.

"Is that your father's?" he asked.

Cywan nodded. "It's his

slingshot," he said. "He could take down a bird in flight from fifty paces."

Frankie had an idea. "May I borrow it?" he asked.

Cywan handed it over. It was a simple design, a pouch and two strips for handles. Frankie lowered it to Max's nose. "Here's your scent, boy — think you can find him?"

"I'll do my best," said Max.

He scampered off, nose to the ground.

Frankie and the others fanned out a little, but stayed in sight of one another. They began to call Cywan's father's name, Brux, but as time went on and their voices wore out, Frankie felt desperate. He didn't know this land at all. Brux could have travelled miles, in any direction. It was like looking for an ant on a football pitch. And if what Cywan said about wild animals was true . . .

Max yelped. "I've found something!" he barked. A second

later, he scampered up from Frankie's left. "Down here!" he said.

Everyone rushed over, peering down a rocky gully. There must have been a spring nearby, because the rocks were slick with water trickling between them, and there were patches of muddy ground.

"I've got a scent," said Max, "but it's really faint."

"Dad!" cried Cywan, but there was no answer.

He began to scramble down the ravine. "Slow down!" said Louise. "It won't do any good if you injure yourself."

They trod carefully, helping each other over difficult sections. The gully widened, and the water flow became a stream. Suddenly Cywan crouched and picked up a small stick. "My father's blow-pipe!" he said, holding it out. "He must have come this way!"

Frankie saw the stick was perfectly straight and hollowed out. He guessed they used it to blow sharpened darts at small prey such as rodents and birds.

"I wonder why he dropped it," said Charlie.

"Maybe because he was being chased!" said Louise. She was a few paces away, standing over a print in the mud. Frankie saw at once that it wasn't made by a human foot. The print had five toes and what might have been long claws.

"A bear!" said Cywan, face bloodless.

Frankie didn't know what to say. *It's not looking good.*

They walked on, descending further into the valley, rounding corners as the gully switched back and forth. Frankie dreaded finding Brux around each new bend, or seeing blood on the stones. Max was darting this way and that, paws scrambling over the slick rocks and through the water. Frankie's feet were cold and sore — he wasn't used to walking shoeless for so long.

Eventually, Max lifted his nose from the ground and said sadly, "I've lost the scent."

Then Frankie spotted a few stems of broken grass. It was a trail, leading up the slope away from the stream. He headed that way at a light jog.

"Where are you going?" asked Louise.

"Brux?" Frankie bellowed, his voice croaky.

He listened for a moment, and

on the wind he was sure he heard something.

As he reached the top of the slope, breathing hard, he saw there was more damaged vegetation. He stopped, reeling, as the ground dropped away on the other side. One more step and he would have fallen over a small bluff.

And there, lying at the bottom, was a man.

CHAPTER 5

Frankie's heart did a flip of fear. The man wasn't moving.

But then he did, shifting on to his elbow as he stared up. "Help me!" he called. "I'm trapped."

"Dad!" cried Cywan, rushing to Frankie's side. They were soon joined by the others.

"Son!" called back Brux. He looked puzzled but relieved.

Frankie looked around, and saw a way down into the dip fifty metres to his right, where the ground levelled off. It took a little bit of scrambling, but soon they reached Brux's side. He was a large man, with a thick beard and shaggy hair. His left leg was trapped under a boulder.

Cywan gave him a huge hug.

"We thought wild animals had got you," he said.

"They almost did!" said Brux. "I came across a bear with her cubs and she chased me. But when I fell down here, she gave up. I was unlucky – my fall disturbed several rocks and this one landed on my leg."

Frankie looked at the rock. It was the size of a beach ball.

"We need to move it — it might be painful."

"I stopped feeling the pain long ago," said Brux. "Do what you must."

Frankie marshalled the others into position on one side of the rock. He doubted they could lift it, so they'd have to roll it off.

"After three," he said, then counted down.

On their mark, everyone heaved. Frankie felt his elbows and shoulders straining almost to snapping, then the rock shifted and rolled clear.

"Ouch!" said Charlie, glancing at

the wound. Brux's shin was gashed badly, the blood dry. His knee was swollen. "I will live," said Cywan's father. "It's nothing old Olsa can't fix. Who are your friends, son?" asked Brux.

Cywan introduced them, leaving Max until last.

"Glad I could help," said the dog.

Brux gaped. "You are not what I thought the Great Spirit or his helpers would be like," he said in awe.

"Don't let size fool you," said Max. "I can catch Frisbees, open the fridge door, and run faster than any postman."

"You speak of things I do not understand, Great Spirit," said Brux. "But I will be forever grateful."

"We need to get you home!" said Cywan. "Mum's so worried. And Tash and Jeri and Rai."

"You'll have to help me stand," said Brux.

With Frankie on one side, and Cywan on the other, they hoisted Brux to his feet. He was heavy, but he could put weight on his good leg. Frankie could see from the sweat pouring off the man's brow that he was in a lot of pain, but trying not to let it show.

They took it in turns to support him, and it was tough going back to the path, but Frankie couldn't stop smiling. *We did it!*

The sun was high in the sky by the time they reached the camp once more. All of Cywan's family came running from the cave to greet

Brux, and there were many hugs
and tears of happiness. As he told
his tale, and the old lady went to
work cleaning his wound, Rai came
over holding the magic football.

"What is this thing?" he asked,
turning it over.

Frankie took it from him and
dropped it to the floor. "It's called
a football," he said. He did a few
keepie-uppies, then flicked the ball
to Louise, who chested it down
and volleyed it towards Charlie. He
leapt up and snatched it from the
air.

Rai looked on amazed. "This
football – is it a spiritual ritual?"

Frankie grinned. "Some people take it very seriously, I suppose."

He wished he could stay and play a proper game with the cave folk, but his mind went to their dads. They'd be worried sick by now. And their job here was done.

"I'd love to stay," he said, "but we have to go back to where we belong."

"Through the stone circle?" said Cywan.

Frankie nodded.

"Can we come and watch?" asked Rai.

"I don't see why not," said Louise.

"You need to stay put," said Olsa

to Brux. "But the rest of you can go."

Frankie said farewell to the old woman and Cywan's mother and father, and followed the others back up to the stone circle.

"That was some adventure," he said to his friends. "I never thought I'd visit the Stone Age!"

"I never thought I'd be called a Great Spirit, either!" said Max. "I think it suits me."

They stopped at the edge of the stone circle, and Frankie kicked the ball into the centre. When it landed, the ground swallowed it up. Everyone gasped as the black hole reappeared.

"Stay back," said Jeri. "It's spirit magic!"

Frankie turned to Cywan, unsure of how to say goodbye. Just as he opened his mouth, a tremendous blaring sound echoed across the hillside.

"That was the horn!" said Tash. "There's trouble back at the cave!"

Frankie looked at his friends, then at the portal.

"We can't leave now!" said Louise, as Cywan ran off towards the cave with his siblings.

The sound of grunts and bellows and human cries drifted to Frankie's ears.

"What do we do?" asked Charlie.

Frankie didn't answer, because his feet were already carrying him after Cywan.

As they broke through the trees, Frankie was confronted with a wall of smelly fur, and the ground shook beneath his feet.

A woolly mammoth, as big as a bus, was stampeding across the clearing. He jumped back as another pounded into view. And a third, smaller one, which must have been a baby.

A baby as big as an elephant, with tusks a metre long.

PART TWO

CHAPTER 6

The ground was vibrating so hard
that Frankie struggled to stay on
his feet. Ashes from the fire flew
into the sky as the mammoths
rampaged over the remains of the
hearth. Bowls and cups and clothes
were being trampled into the
ground.

"Get back!" cried Brux. He'd
grabbed a spear and was jabbing

at the nearest mammoth, hobbling around on his injured leg.

"Everyone else, in the cave!" called Olsa. The children were squealing as they clung to their mother.

Then Frankie saw Tash trip and fall. One of the mammoths was rushing towards her. "Help me, Great Spirit!" she shouted.

"I think she means you," said Charlie to Max.

"Oh, yes . . . right," said Max. He bounded underneath another mammoth's legs, and rushed to intercept the charging creature. He planted his feet and barked wildly, snarling.

He's going to get himself crushed, thought Frankie.

But the mammoth skidded to a stop, rearing up on its hind legs.

Max advanced, and the mammoth backed away.

"Great work, boy!" called Frankie. He saw Louise help Tash to her feet and rush to the cave. The mammoths stomped out of the clearing, smashing through the trees and leaving devastation in their wake. Brux was leaning heavily on his spear.

"The Great Spirit saved us once more!" he gasped.

Max wagged his tail. "Think nothing of it."

Charlie stooped and picked up the mammoth horn in both hands. "At least this isn't damaged," he said.

"The main thing is that no one was hurt," said Olsa.

Frankie looked at crushed pots and pans and the remains of the fire. It probably wouldn't take long for them to get back to normal.

"We really should be getting home," he said to his friends.

"I'll stay here this time," said Cywan. "Thank you, Great Spirit. And thank you, Frankie."

Max led the way, head held high. But as they approached the stone circle, Frankie saw the ground here was torn up too. He glanced around nervously. There were several patches of flattened grass, each the size of a dinner plate.

"Uh-oh, I think one of the mammoths might have come this way," he said. "Keep your eyes peeled."

Max sniffed. "Yep, definitely mammoth feet." He kept his nose to the ground.

"Did you know, mammoths were vegetarian?" said Louise.

"I'm not sure we need mammoth facts right now," said Charlie.

"Just saying," muttered Louise. "It won't try and eat us."

"It's not its teeth I'm worried about," said Charlie. "What if it—"

"Oh no!" said Frankie, pulling back his friend. "Look!"

The mammoth was standing dead ahead, tearing at the grass beside the stone circle. Frankie could see the black portal was still there. The giant creature was only a few metres from it.

"OK, everyone," said Frankie. "Whatever you do, don't startle it. We'll just have to wait for it to—"

"Don't worry!" said Max. "Let the Great Spirit handle this." He started to trot forwards.

"No!" they all hissed, but Max wasn't listening.

"Hey, furball!" he called. The mammoth swung its massive head to face him. "Yeah, you," Max continued. "Out of the way!"

The mammoth's eyes widened and it took a few steps back.

"Max, stop!" said Frankie.

Max advanced. "The Great Spirit demands that you move!" he barked.

The mammoth shuffled further away, lifted its trunk and blew out a long, honking sound.

And then it vanished into the ground.

"Oh," said Max.

"It's gone through the portal!" cried Louise.

"After it!" yelled Frankie.

They all ran forwards, and Frankie scooped up Max on the way. The portal in the stone circle was shrinking fast. If they didn't make it, they'd be trapped here forever.

Frankie jumped towards the black circle, and the sky above him disappeared.

The first thing he saw on the other side was Kevin curled in a ball and wailing, with the magic football beside him. He rushed over to his brother. "Are you hurt?" he asked.

Kevin peered through his fingers, his face pale. "Is it gone? The elephant?"

Frankie helped his brother up. For once, he actually felt a little sorry for him. "For a start, it's a mammoth," he said. "And yes."

"The question is, where?" said Louise.

"I don't understand," said Kevin. "Where did you find an elephant . . . I mean a mammoth?"

"In the Stone Age, obviously," said Charlie. He pointed with his gloved hand at a flattened hedge. "I think it went through there."

Frankie groaned. On the other

side, he saw the mammoth drinking from a water trough without a care in the world. Looking at the sky, he realised it was late afternoon.

"Hang on — have you been here for a whole day?" asked Frankie. "Aren't our dads worried?"

"What are you talking about?" said Kevin, frowning. "You've been gone about two minutes."

Thank goodness for that, thought Frankie. *At least we haven't completely ruined the trip. Yet.*

"How are we going to get two tonnes of mammoth back to the stone circle?" asked Louise.

We need to act fast, thought Frankie. *People could be hurt.*

"We need a leash," he said. "A big one ... "

"How about a rope?" said Charlie. "My dad keeps one in the car boot in case we have to be towed!"

Frankie clicked his fingers. "Great thinking! Kev and Charlie, you stay here. Louise and I will go and get the rope."

"What are we supposed to do?" asked Kevin.

"Make sure it doesn't go anywhere," said Louise.

Kevin opened his mouth to say something, but then just nodded weakly.

Charlie went to the gap in the hedge, and stared at his goalie gloves. "Nothing gets past me."

Frankie took off with Louise, back towards the campsite. As they neared the tents, he smelled cooking meat on the barbecue and saw Louise and Charlie's dads. He couldn't see his own. *This was supposed to be about us spending time with our dads, but now it's turning into a prehistoric catastrophe.*

He put his finger to his lips and they sneaked around the back of the tents to where the people carrier was parked. With Louise on lookout duty, Frankie cracked open the boot. It was still full of stuff, but he rooted around and found a coil of green rope. It looked strong, but would it be strong enough? He was about to take it out when he heard his dad's voice.

"Frankie, what *are* you doing?"

CHAPTER 7

Frankie's heart sank and he turned slowly. His dad had come from the other direction, and he was carrying a bottle of ketchup, no doubt bought from the site shop.

"I ... er ... I just came to see if Charlie's gloves were in here."

His dad frowned. "They're probably on his hands, aren't they? I'm not sure I've ever seen his hands without them! Anyway, what's the rope for?"

Frankie felt himself blushing. He hated not telling his dad the truth, but he could hardly say he needed the rope to contain an escaped mammoth.

Louise came to his rescue. "A

rope swing!" she said. "We're going to build a rope swing in the forest."

"Is it safe?" asked his dad.

"Oh yes!" said Louise. "We'll be really careful."

Frankie thought his dad was going to tell them to put it back, but in the end he nodded. All grown-ups trusted Louise. "All right then," he said. "But the food will be ready in twenty minutes." He grinned. "If you're not careful, the oldies will eat all the sausages."

"We'll be quick," said Frankie.

He headed back towards the stone circle. On the way, he tried to remember the knot his dad had shown him before — the one like a lasso. It took a couple of goes, but eventually he got it right.

Tossing it over the mammoth's head might prove trickier, he thought.

By the time they reached the stone circle again, Louise was ahead, looking around and frowning. "Where are they?" she said.

Frankie couldn't see Charlie, Max, or Kevin anywhere.

"Perhaps they managed to coax it back already?" Frankie said.

"How?" said Louise. "The portal's closed."

Then the ground began to shake and they heard panicked barking.

"Move!" yelled Charlie.

Frankie spun around as Charlie came charging through the gap in the hedge with Kevin. Max scampered at their side.

And behind them came about fifty cows, eyes rolling wildly as they thundered from the field.

And behind *them* charged the mammoth.

Frankie grabbed Louise and tugged her aside. The sound of the herd careering past was deafening. They bellowed and mooed and snorted. Kevin and Charlie scrambled up the nearest tree, and Max jumped into Louise's arms.

The cows ran past, charging towards the woods. "They're heading for the campsite," said Louise.

As the mammoth approached, Frankie hurled the lasso. It slipped over one of the creature's tusks.

"Great shot!" said Charlie.

But the mammoth didn't stop, and Frankie was yanked right off his feet. He kept a grip on the rope as he was hauled across the grass.

"Help!" he cried, as he bounced across the ground.

He managed to spin round

and tried to dig his heels into the ground, but the mammoth barely seemed to notice. It hauled Frankie towards the trees. He might as well have been trying to stop a moving car.

"We're coming!" called Louise. But Frankie couldn't hold on any longer, and lost his grip. He sprawled across the ground as Louise and Charlie came running up.

"Are you OK?" asked Charlie.

Frankie looked down at his filthy torn clothes. He was covered in scratches and scrapes as well. "Just about," he said.

"We tried to stop it," said Charlie.

"I think it just wanted to make friends with the cows."

They didn't need Max's nose to track the mammoth this time. Frankie followed the trail of churned-up ground and broken branches. There were cows wandering aimlessly under the trees, but no sign of the mammoth.

"I think we're heading away from the campsite," said Charlie breathlessly.

But as they emerged from the cover of the trees, Frankie saw they were still in a lot of trouble. They weren't near the tents, but below were rows and rows of caravans.

"Where's it gone?" said Louise.

Suddenly, one of the caravans rocked to one side. Then another. Frankie saw a flash of brown hair as the mammoth romped between them.

Doors flew open and people came out, looking around.

Frankie looked at his friends, then they all began to run.

If we don't capture that mammoth, someone might be killed!

CHAPTER 8

By the time they reached the caravans, several dozen people had emerged from inside. They were talking about earthquakes and hurricanes, and looking very confused. Two caravans had actually been knocked off their moorings, and leaned over at an angle. As far as Frankie could see, no one was hurt, thank goodness.

Above the hubbub of voices, he couldn't hear the sound of the mammoth's pounding feet.

"Where's it gone now?" he muttered.

With his friends, they left the bystanders and crept between the caravans.

He wondered where he'd go, if he were a mammoth on the loose in a strange world. And then he smelled something. Something *horrible*.

Louise and Charlie were screwing up their faces too.

As they rounded a caravan, Frankie came face to face with

an enormous pile of steaming, football-sized balls of dung. Flies buzzed around it.

"I guess it came this way," said Charlie, pulling his T-shirt over his nose.

"There's more up ahead!" said Louise, pointing.

They followed the trail, then Frankie saw a fence had been knocked down. Some orangey hair was tangled on a fallen post, and he could hear snorting beyond, coming from a thicket of undergrowth and stunted trees.

He put a finger to his lips and beckoned the others.

"Hey, wait for me!" said Kevin. He came hobbling over, holding the magic football. Frankie normally would have told him to hand it over, but now they had bigger problems.

They climbed over the remains of the fence, and through the long grass on the other side. The ground sloped downwards into a small valley. It squelched under Frankie's feet, and soon there was mud all up his ankles.

"Yuck!" said Kevin.

They picked their way between the trees and thorny tendrils, and finally saw the mammoth. It was standing up to its belly in a muddy

pond, looking quite pleased with
itself. The rope still trailed from
its tusk. Then it lifted its trunk and
blasted a spray of brown liquid over
its back, and over Kevin. He let out
a squeal of disgust. The mammoth
turned on them, eyes rolling in
panic.

Frankie held up both hands. "It's all right," he said soothingly. "We're your friends."

"I'm not!" said Kevin, wiping mud from his eyes.

The mammoth whipped the scummy pond's surface with its trunk, then it began to stride towards Frankie's brother. Kevin froze, knees trembling.

"Run!" said Louise.

But Kevin didn't even seem to hear her. His terrified gaze was fixed on the advancing beast, then he clamped his eyes closed, dropped the football, and waited to be squished. Frankie grabbed the

rope, but he knew he didn't have a chance of stopping the mammoth on his own. Then he spotted a tree stump nearby. The mammoth charged at Kevin, just as Frankie looped the end of the rope — once, twice, three times — around the stump. Then he braced himself. The rope went taut, and the mammoth stopped a few paces short of Kevin. It yanked again, shaking its head, but the rope held, tightening around the stump.

Charlie and Louise each grabbed Kevin's arms and pulled him out of the way.

But what now? thought Frankie.

"We need to get back to the stone circle," he said.

Max began to bark from the bushes. He stuck his head out, tongue lolling, and vanished back into the thicket. "What's up with him?" asked Louise.

She waded through the shallows of the pool, and stuck her head through the gap where Max had disappeared. "Oh my!" she said.

Frankie kept one eye on the mammoth straining against the rope as he went over too. Pushing aside some branches, he found Louise and Charlie standing beside a dark hole in the hillside surrounded by rocks and clumps of dry earth.

"I think the mammoth must have caused a landslip," said Louise.

"Maybe it's an old mine shaft," said Charlie, joining them with a mud-spattered Kevin.

Frankie felt a strange tickle across the back of his neck. There was something familiar about where they were standing, and the shape of the cave mouth. The truth hit him.

He looked around, trying to get his bearings.

"I think this is Cywan's cave!" he said.

The sound of adult voices reached Frankie's ears. "Is anybody down there?"

And another. "Has anyone seen four kids and a dog?" Frankie recognised his dad's voice.

"Charlie?" shouted his father.

Louise's eyes went wide. "Uh-oh — the grown-ups are coming!"

Frankie looked into the cave. They could hide themselves, but what about the mammoth? As soon as their fathers reached the pond, they could hardly not notice it!

There's nothing we can do.

"I've got an idea!" said Kevin. He turned and ran off.

Typical! thought Frankie. *Leaving us to face the music.*

A few seconds later, he returned, carrying the magic football. "Could we use this? You know, to create one of those magic doorways."

"I don't think even Frankie can kick it all the way to the stone circle from here," said Louise.

"Not the stone circle," said Kevin. "The cave!"

Louise's dad's voice shouted. "I think they came this way!"

"It's got to be worth a try," said Frankie. He took the ball from his brother, and kicked it into the cave mouth. He heard it bounce once in the darkness, then nothing.

"So much for that idea," said Charlie.

Frankie's heart sank. They were seconds from being discovered. What a disaster. *This really can't get any worse.*

But then it did, because they all heard the loud *twang* of a snapping rope.

The mammoth was on the loose again.

CHAPTER 9

Two massive tusks tore the vegetation aside, and the mammoth's head appeared. As soon as it set its eyes on them, it bellowed and charged.

With nowhere else to go, Frankie and his friends ran into the cave and the gloom swallowed them.

Frankie couldn't see more than a couple of metres ahead, but he could hear the pounding of the mammoth's feet, and feel its huge shadow at his back. He threw out his hands, expecting at any moment to hit the dead end of the back of the cave. But he didn't. Charlie and Louise and Kevin ran at his side, with Max just ahead.

Soon there was no light at all, and he was running blind, with only the sounds of his friends' heavy breaths and scuffing of their feet. He realised he couldn't hear the pursuing mammoth any more, and slowed.

"This cave is enormous!" whispered Louise.

Almost impossibly enormous, thought Frankie. *Magically enormous, even ...*

"Hey — I think I see a light," said Charlie. Frankie felt a glove grip his arm and pull him along. Then he saw it too — a faint arc of daylight in the distance. Had they somehow followed a path back to the entrance? He didn't think so. *We ran in a straight line ...*

They all wandered together towards it.

Frankie felt dizzy as they emerged into the open landscape, but it wasn't the thicket near the campsite. Cywan and his family were stacking wood and sweeping up broken pottery.

"You're back!" Cywan said.

"So we are," said Frankie, gazing all around. Kevin looked sick with fear.

"We wondered where this came from," said Cywan. He had the magic football under his foot.

So it did *work!* thought Frankie.

But where was the . . .

"Mammoth!" cried Tasha, pointing right at Frankie.

He spun around and saw the creature rushing from the depths of the cave. He and Charlie leapt one way, Kevin and Louise the other, as

the mammoth burst from the cave mouth. It skidded to a halt, and lifted its trunk in a mighty bellow that shook the ground. No one even had time to grab a spear. But a few seconds later, another mammoth replied with an echoing cry in the distance. The huge beast swung its head from side to side, then trampled off across the clearing and into the trees. They all watched it go, speechless. Well, all except for Max, who marched to the edge of the clearing and barked after it. "And don't come back, or you'll have me to answer to!"

Cywan and his family laughed.

"I think it just wanted its mum," said Louise.

"I know how it feels," muttered Kevin. He goggled at the Stone Age people. "What is this place?"

"Are you one of the Great Spirit's servants too?" asked Osha.

"The Great Who?" said Kevin.

Max trotted back, tail held high. "She means me," he said.

"Your *servant*?" scoffed Kevin. "I think you'll find it's the other way around. He's just a dog, you know? A pretty disobedient one, actually."

Cywan's people looked at Kevin like he was mad. But it was Brux who hobbled forward on a crutch. "You must all stay for a feast," he said. He glared at Kevin. "Even the one who disrespects the Great Spirit."

Frankie's stomach rumbled. He realised he hadn't eaten anything since lunch time, and that seemed a long, long time ago. But they had to get back. Even though the hours here passed differently, their dads were looking for them now. They'd sounded really worried.

"Thank you for the offer," said Frankie, "but we have to leave."

Cywan looked at the floor sadly.

"Will we ever see you again?" he asked.

Frankie didn't want to disappoint him. "I suppose there's a chance we'll come back — one day."

"Don't worry," said Max, placing a paw on Cywan's leg. "The Great Spirit will always be watching over you."

"Oh, please!" said Kevin. "This is ridiculous. Hey, kid." He walked towards Cywan. "Hand over the ball."

But as he tried to kick it from under Cywan's foot, the young boy rolled it back neatly and Kevin fell over on his bum.

"You're learning already," said
Louise.

Kevin, red-faced, picked himself
up. "Very funny."

Cywan passed the ball to Frankie.

"Thank you again for rescuing my
father," he said. "We will remember
this day always."

"Ha!" said Charlie. "You could even call it Father's Day."

"What a good idea!" said Cywan.

Frankie walked back to the cave, then kicked the ball inside. It vanished.

"Goodbye!" he said, waving.

The Stone Age family waved back.

"Happy Father's Day," said Cywan.

Frankie led his friends into the darkness, and felt the magic of the football all around him.

CHAPTER 10

A bright light made Frankie screw up his eyes.

"Frankie!" said his dad.

More torch-beams lit up the darkness of the cave. One by one, more grown-ups gathered around. Louise's dad wrapped her in his arms, and Charlie's dad grabbed his son in a tight embrace.

"We've been looking everywhere

for you!" he said. "We thought you might have been injured in the earthquake."

"What earthquake?" asked Frankie, as his dad led him outside.

"Are you kidding? Where have you been?"

Frankie saw the others all watching him. There was someone in a park ranger uniform, too. He noticed a trail of rope on the floor, with a frayed end.

"We were building a rope swing," he said. "We stumbled on this cave."

The ranger frowned. "I'm pretty sure this landslip wasn't even here yesterday. Oh my! You could have been badly hurt."

"You know kids," said Louise's dad. "Always exploring!"

The ranger nodded. "Well, they're lucky," he said. "We'll have to get a warning sign up so no one else comes this way. Anyway, I've got a mountain of dung to clear up."

"Really?" said Louise.

"Hmm," said the ranger. "It looks like a herd of cows somehow got into the caravan park. Don't suppose you know anything about that?"

Louise shook her head vigorously.

"Hey!" said Charlie's dad. "Have

you seen in here?" He was standing in the cave mouth, torch flashing across the ceiling. "There are loads of drawings!"

The ranger scowled. "Not graffiti, I hope."

Charlie's dad was open-mouthed. He shook his head.

One by one, they drifted to his side, and the other grown-ups flicked on their torch-beams too. Frankie gasped.

"That's not graffiti," muttered Louise.

The cave walls and ceiling were covered in paintings directly on the surfaces of rock. Herds of bison, horses galloping, wolves and mammoths, all in beautiful detail and natural colours.

"My word!" said Louise's dad. "I think these might be prehistoric cave paintings."

Frankie's dad called out, "There are more, over here." He shone his torch on a number of handprints.

The ranger was shaking his head in amazement. "Do you realise – you kids might have stumbled on one of the greatest archaeological finds in modern times? Whoever drew these must have worshipped at the stone circle."

Frankie saw the grin spread

across Louise's face and smiled back. Over her shoulder his eyes fell on another image. Four figures with what looked like a dog and a small circle floating above them, like a football flying through the air.

I wonder if Cywan drew that one . . .

"We should go now," said the ranger. "I need to contact the owner and let him know about this. The whole place will need to be sealed off until the experts get here."

Frankie would have liked to stay for longer, taking in the amazing drawings, but he knew the ranger

was right. He was about to leave when Charlie's dad exclaimed, "Look at the size of this print. Whoever left it must have been a giant!" He shone his torch on a particularly large handprint in red paint.

Frankie saw Charlie glance at his goalie glove, covered in the same colour, then quickly shove it behind his back. Louise must have seen too, because she chuckled.

They emerged back into the scrubby undergrowth, and slowly climbed the slope back towards the caravan park.

People were all out of their

caravans and tents, chatting to one another. And soon the news about the amazing cave began to spread as the sun set across the site.

The ranger talked excitedly on his phone about the discovery. Frankie heard him saying. "No – just kids! Unbelievable."

You don't know the half of it, he thought.

Frankie would never forget his adventure in the Stone Age, meeting Cywan and his family, but it felt great to be back with his dad again. He was looking forward to doing something normal for the rest of the weekend.

As they walked towards their tent, Kevin caught up with him.

"I'm sorry I took your football," he said.

Frankie was flabbergasted. He wasn't sure his brother had ever actually said "sorry" to him before.

"That's all right," he said. "It was a bit of a crazy adventure, wasn't it?"

Kevin blew out his cheeks. "You can say that again." He picked a long coarse mammoth hair off Frankie's arm and tossed it in the grass.

Their dad came up behind them and put his hands on each of their shoulders. "I was really worried about you guys," he said. "No more straying over fences, OK? Just stick to something safer from now on. Football, or something like that. You can't get into bother kicking a football around, can you?"

Frankie heard his brother snigger, and he burst out laughing too.

"What's so funny?" asked his dad.

"Nothing," said Frankie. "Nothing at all."

ACKNOWLEDGEMENTS

Many thanks to everyone at Hachette Children's Group; Neil Blair, Zoe King, Daniel Teweles and all at The Blair Partnership; Luella Wright for bringing my characters to life; special thanks to Michael Ford for all his wisdom and patience; and to Steve Kutner for being a great friend and for all his help and guidance, not just with the book but with everything.

Turn the page for
a sneak peek at
Frankie's next adventure,
Summer Holiday Showdown,
coming soon!

Frankie and his friends have been transported back in time to a boarding school by the magic football, but they're not sure why. Then they meet George and think they must have been sent to help him – but George doesn't seem so sure ...

George bowled Frankie over and they hit the ground hard. Frankie tried to squirm out, but George was stronger than he looked. "Give it to me!" he yelled.

Eventually, Charlie and Louise hoisted the smaller boy off. His face was wild, and he continued to struggle against them. "Calm down!" Frankie urged.

Slowly, George ran out of steam, and hung limply between Charlie and Louise, his chest heaving.

"I need to have the magic football," he sobbed.

"Wait – *what*?" said Frankie. "How do you know it's magic?"

George glanced sorrowfully and Charlie, then Louise. "You can let me go," he said.

Frankie's friends looked to Frankie, who nodded. George sat

down on the edge of a bed, with his shoulders slumped.

"You said the football belonged to you," said Charlie. "How is that possible?"

"My brother and I were at a different school before we got sent here. We both loved playing football. We found the ball at the back of the sports cupboard when we were sneaking around. And then we learned of its powers. We used to go on adventures together, until . . ." He trailed off.

"Until what?" asked Louise gently.

"Alex was older than me," said George. "We used to argue a lot.

One time, we disagreed about using the football. I said we should take a break, he didn't want to. Then, one day about a month ago, he was gone."

George looked close to tears again.

"So he didn't run away from school," said Frankie.

George shook his head. "No. I could hardly tell everyone he'd gone through a magical doorway."

"I think the magic football brought us here to help you," said Frankie. "If you'll let us?"

"Help *me*?" said George, his face brightening. "Why would you?"

"Because it's the right thing to do," said Louise. "Have you any idea where Alex might be?"

"Yes!" George hopped off the bed, and went to his chest of drawers. He pulled one out completely then flipped it over on the bed, spilling the clothes. Taped to the underside was a piece of parchment paper, discoloured with age. There were markings on it.

"A map!" said Charlie. "It looks really old."

They crowded closer. Frankie saw it was an island, and there was an X marked on it.

"It's a treasure map," said George. "We won it from a bunch of real pirates on one of our adventures."

Frankie smiled. They'd faced some pirates too once – and almost been fed to the sharks!

"I think Alex went looking for the treasure," said George. "But he must have failed, because he never came back. Nor did the ball, until now."

Frankie smiled and said, "let's find Alex."

George nodded, and fished out the map. Then he held out a hand for the football. "May I?"

Frankie handed it over. With the map on the floor, George held the football over the top. "Ready?" he said.

Frankie and his friends gathered around.

George dropped the football, but when it hit the map, it fell straight through, vanishing. The floorboards under their feet went soft like jelly, then all around the walls dissolved. Frankie felt a warm breeze gusting against his skin, and squinted against a bright light.

When he could see again, the dormitory had vanished, and he was standing on a stretch of white sand, with palm trees rising all around, under a cloudless blue sky. Waves sloshed against the shore. Frankie turned on the spot, hand up to shield his eyes. All he saw was clear ocean stretching to the horizon . . .

FRANKIE'S MAGIC FOOTBALL WEBSITE

Have you had a chance to check out
frankiesmagicfootball.co.uk yet?

Get involved in **competitions**, find out **news** and
updates about the series, play **games** and watch
videos featuring the author, **Frank Lampard!**

Visit the site to join
Frankie's FC today!